Fungus the Bogeyman

RAYMOND BRIGGS

Fungus the Bogeyman

BOGEYDOM
is dark, dim, unclear, indefinite
indistinct, abstruse, difficult to understand,
unexplained, doubtful, hidden, secluded,
remote from public observation, unknown,
lowly, humble, dull, dingy, gloomy, murky....
NOW READ ON ⟹

PENGUIN BOOKS

Fungus the Bogeyman

The Sun sinks below the hills. The birds are hushed.
NIGHT is coming.
BUT......far, far below.....in THE TUNNELS
in the wet, dripping tunnels of Bogeydom,
(a land where the light is as Darkness)
the Bogeymen are stirring in their beds....
The roofs of the houses are wet,
the walls are slimy and dank.
A damp chill hangs in the air.
   Now, as the last light fades from THE TUNNELS,
   it is the black dawn of a new Bogey day......

Time to get up, Fungus my dreary*.
It's nearly dark.

MMMMM......
ZZZZZZ....

*dreary: Bogish for dear, deary

OOOH! What a night that was!
This bed has almost dried up!

I know, drear.
It needs more slime.

What a horrible day!
Feels quite warm!

I hate this time of year.
It's so light.

Ah!
Nice wet dressing-gown and sabots!

I'll change the sheets today, drear.
The dirt has almost worn off these.

I know, love, the smell's all gone

HERE WE RAISE THE COVERS TO DISCLOSE THE HORRORS WHICH LURK IN THE FETID DARKNESS BENEATH

BOGEYBEDS
Slugs and hodmandods* are tolerated and even encouraged in Bogeybeds. These creatures produce the silvery slime which Bogeymen find so delicious against their skins.
A well-looked-after Bogeybed will contain anything up to two hundred slugs and hodmandods. Inevitably, some of these will be crushed when the Bogey turns over, but these losses are soon made good as there are always eggs in the corners of the bed.
   The slug or snail corpse is never removed but if large pieces of shell irritate the Bogey's sensitive skin, they will be carefully picked out and eaten. The soft jelly remaining is thought by Bogeys to add to the richness and 'slime-savour' of the bed.
   *hodmandods: snails

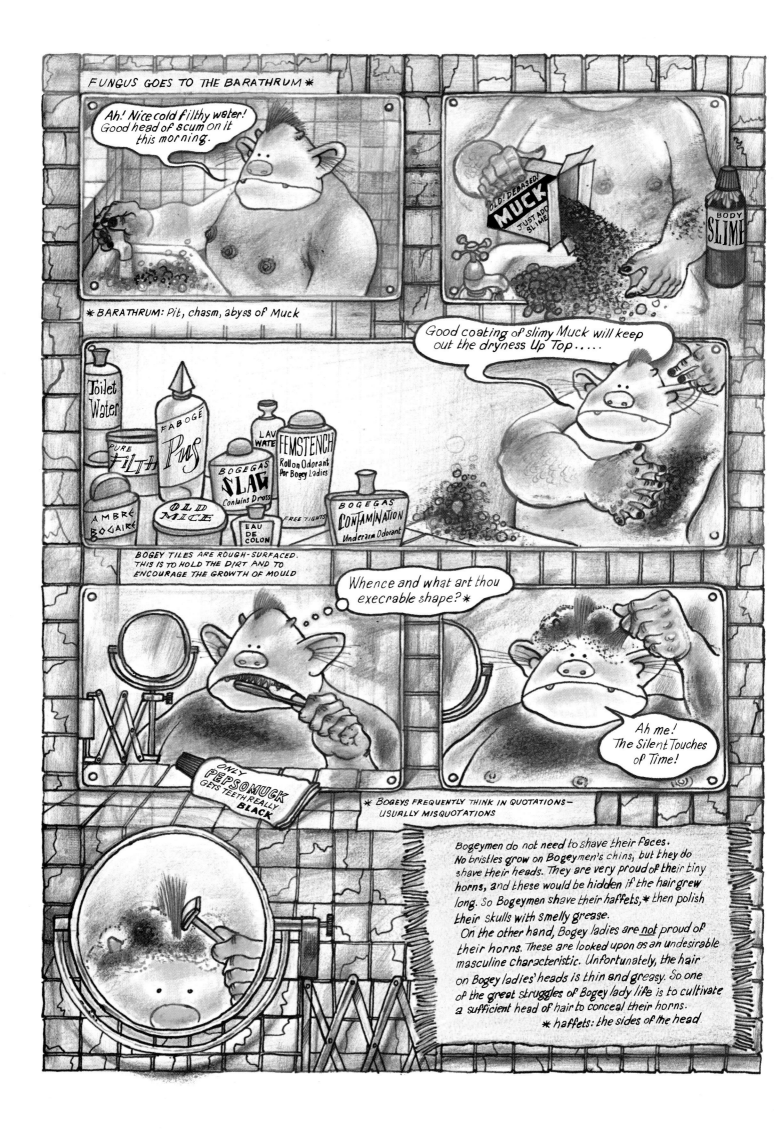

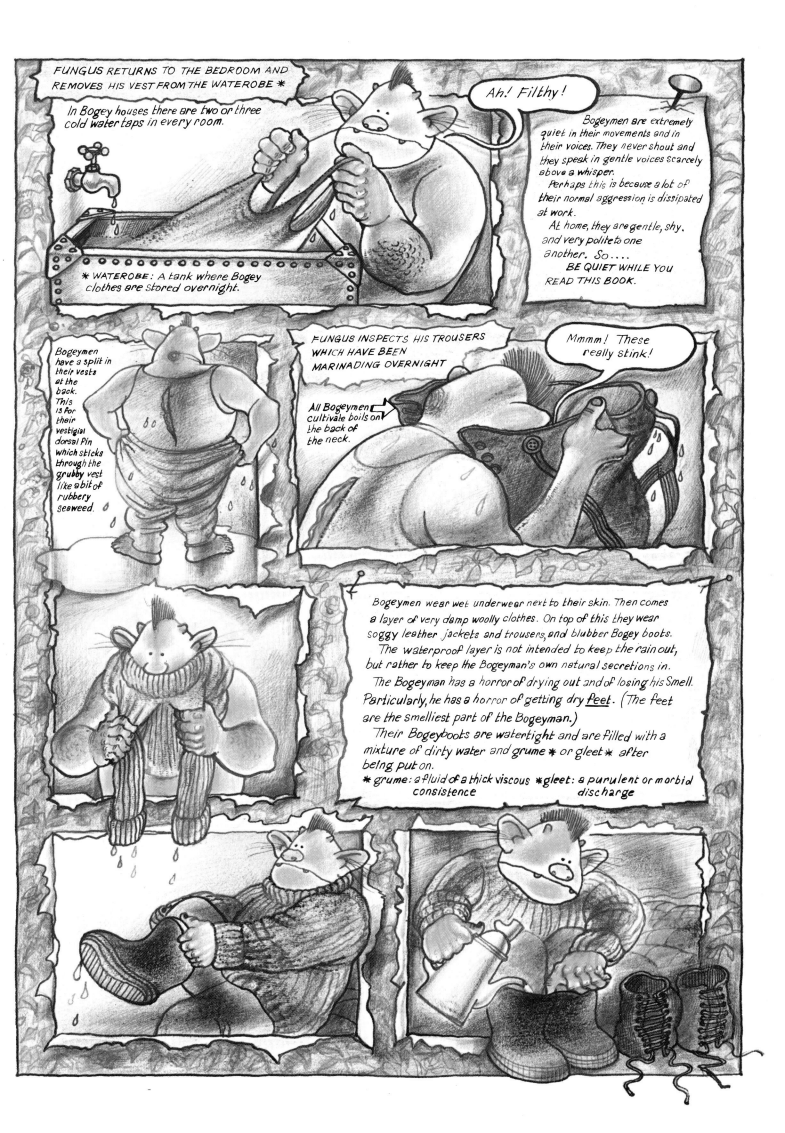

FUNGUS RETURNS TO THE BEDROOM AND REMOVES HIS VEST FROM THE WATEROBE *

In Bogey houses there are two or three cold water taps in every room.

* WATEROBE: A tank where Bogey clothes are stored overnight.

Ah! Filthy!

Bogeymen are extremely quiet in their movements and in their voices. They never shout and they speak in gentle voices scarcely above a whisper.
 Perhaps this is because a lot of their normal aggression is dissipated at work.
 At home, they are gentle, shy, and very polite to one another. So....
 BE QUIET WHILE YOU READ THIS BOOK.

Bogeymen have a split in their vests at the back. This is for their vestigial dorsal fin which sticks through the grubby vest like a bit of rubbery seaweed.

FUNGUS INSPECTS HIS TROUSERS WHICH HAVE BEEN MARINADING OVERNIGHT

All Bogeymen cultivate boils on the back of the neck.

Mmmm! These really stink!

Bogeymen wear wet underwear next to their skin. Then comes a layer of very damp woolly clothes. On top of this they wear soggy leather jackets and trousers, and blubber Bogey boots.
 The waterproof layer is not intended to keep the rain out, but rather to keep the Bogeyman's own natural secretions in.
 The Bogeyman has a horror of drying out and of losing his Smell. Particularly, he has a horror of getting dry feet. (The feet are the smelliest part of the Bogeyman.)
 Their Bogeyboots are watertight and are filled with a mixture of dirty water and grume * or gleet * after being put on.
* grume: a fluid of a thick viscous consistence
* gleet: a purulent or morbid discharge

Hear that, son? Mind you wrap up well or you'll get dry — Here Mildew, look. This milk's not solid yet — It's still white.

OK Dad.

I must speak to that milkman.

YOUR GUARANTEE OF IMPURITY MILK

Bogey cows are thin, dismal-looking creatures. Hornless and tail-less, they graze on the yellowing grass in the muddy fields. Their watery milk is half-sour when it leaves the cow and by the time it has been delivered it is clotting and turning a pale green. This is how Bogeymen like it. All Bogey cows (and most other cows) are polygastric[1] poephagus[2] poleys.[3]

BOGEY NEWSPAPERS
All Bogeys are misoneists (those who hate anything new.) Consequently, they do not like "news". They prefer "olds". All the information in Bogey oldspapers is guaranteed to be at least one year old. The older the information the more highly Bogeys value it.

However, Bogeys are usually too apathetic to take an interest in important events, no matter how old, so their oldspapers are filled with "strip cartoons" — (a form of entertainment for the simple-minded) which has a large and devoted following in Bogeydom, and "stick-ups". ✱

Bogey stick-ups present an interesting contrast to "pin-ups," as Bogeymen like their stick-ups to be pictures of fat, ugly, heavily-clothed, old Bogey women.

✱ stick-ups: pin-ups. Bogey newspapers are so wet, and Bogey wells so mucky, no pins are needed.

Sully Sloven: (88-93-99) Grey-haired Sully is 84. Her favourite colour is bile green and her favourite pets are her twenty-seven sewer-rats.

LATER

Oooh! What a lovely egg, drear! Really ripe and fuscous ✱ Mmmm, the smell!

Well, I'd better be off, Mildew my love.

Take care, Fungus my darkling. Try not to get your feet dry.

Give us a nice slimy kiss, drear.

✱fuscous: brown tinged with black or grey

✱Boibye, Sourheart. Boibye, Fungus love....

SMELL THIS HOUSE

Boibye Mould.

I'll glaur✱ the bar muffs on the Bogeybike, Dad.

✱ Boibye: corruption of "Boils be with you"

✱glaur: to make muddy

1 polygastric: having many stomachs   2 poephagus: subsisting on grass   3 poleys: hornless (of cattle)

BAR MUFFS
Filled with Glaur or wet Muck to prevent wind drying the hands

HANDLEBARS
Bogeybikes do not have drop handlebars. Bogeys hate speed

CARRIER (for Bogeybag)
The bag is placed in front so that its odours are wafted back to the Bogey's eager nostrils

STRAPS
To tie down THE THINGS when they wriggle in the bag. (see below)

SOLID WHEELS
Spokes would rust away in the wet Bogey climate

SOFT FAT TYRES
(for slowness) Bogey tyres are filled with TYRE (curdled milk and cream beginning to sour)

BUMMLE TANK
An extra tank used to replenish the Bummle-boiler; often needed by the obese Bogey, or Bogeys with exceptionally hot bottoms

WIDE SADDLE
All Bogeys have big fat bottoms

BUMMLE BOILER
A tank of filthy water placed under the saddle where it draws heat from the Bogey's bottom and labouring thighs. This is then converted into steam and discharged rearwards, thus aiding propulsion

BUMMLE DRUM
A muffled drum attached to the saddle. On their long lonely journeys in the Upper Tunnels, Bogeys can be heard desultorily tapping these little drums as they ride

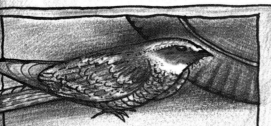

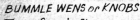

NO MUDGUARDS
Bogeys enjoy being sprayed by wet mud and filth from the road

OIL LAMPIONS
Bogeymen use old-fashioned oil lamps. They cannot bear the hum of a dynamo or the brightness of light from electric batteries. They also enjoy the dirt, mess and smell of oil lamps. Bogeys do not use cheap oil — only the finest Sperm oil

WHEELBIRD
This nocturnal bird inhabits THE TUNNELS and sucks the tyres of Bogeybikes for the curdled milk they contain. This Bogey species is closely related to the Nightjar or Goatsucker

WHEELBUG
These large reduviid insects infest the wheels of Bogeybikes and are often accidentally ground up in the axles to become a sticky substance resembling Jam. Bogeys find this Axlejam particularly delicious

BUMMLE WENS or KNOBS
These fungi often grow on the skirts of unused saddles

BUMMLE EAVES
The jocular name given to the dripping sides of the saddle

BUMMLE OYSTERS
These remarkable striated shellfish are frequently found clustering on the undersides of Bogey bummles

BOGEYBAGS
Every Bogeyman carries a Bogeybag — usually made of damp sacking.
   Sacking is the ideal material for a Bogeybag.
It keeps THE THINGS inside moist.....
   It lets air <u>in</u> so THE THINGS inside can B–R–E–A–T–H–E
It lets moisture <u>out</u> when THE THINGS inside D–R–I–P
and smells from inside can be savoured by
the Bogeyman as he fondles the Bag.....

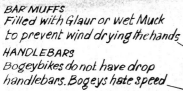

BOGEY BARGE BUSES

In Bogeydom, this land of eternal, dampness, there is no lack of water, and the countryside is criss-crossed by canals. There are no cars in Bogeydom, the Bogey's acute hearing would not tolerate such things, so his love of silence makes water the ideal method of transport. Bogeymen only ride bicycles to work because they have to go uphill to the Surface.

Filthy barges ply the black and stinking canals. Some of these are used for passengers and are treated as buses. The barge buses are towed by Bogey beeves; black, powerful animals with seal-like skins and wide hooves, well-adapted to plodding on the soft mud of the canal banks.

A curious phenomenon is to be noted on the barge buses. Passengers sit in rows on benches in the well of the barge-there are no windows - and if there is a long trip between stops, the Bogeys begin swaying gently and rhythmically together and humming almost inaudibly.

This seems to occur quite unconsciously and with no direction. Although almost inaudible, its effect is quite charming and even magical, and has been known to affect the most prosaic of listeners.

I wonder what It's all FOR?.....
The brimming dykes are not so full
As my heart's silent swell.....

YONDER ALL
BEFORE US LIE
DESERTS OF VAST
ETERNITY

FLYFISHING

Angling for flies with natural or artificial fish as bait.

Flies are one of the great Bogey delights. They are bred commercially and both flies and maggots are sold in shops. Most Bogeys carry a flycase, and the flies or maggots are offered to friends in a similar way to sweets or cigarettes.

There are many different brands, ranging from the common WILLS WOODFLY up to the expensive BALKAN SOBRANIBEE and the strong French GALLWASPS.

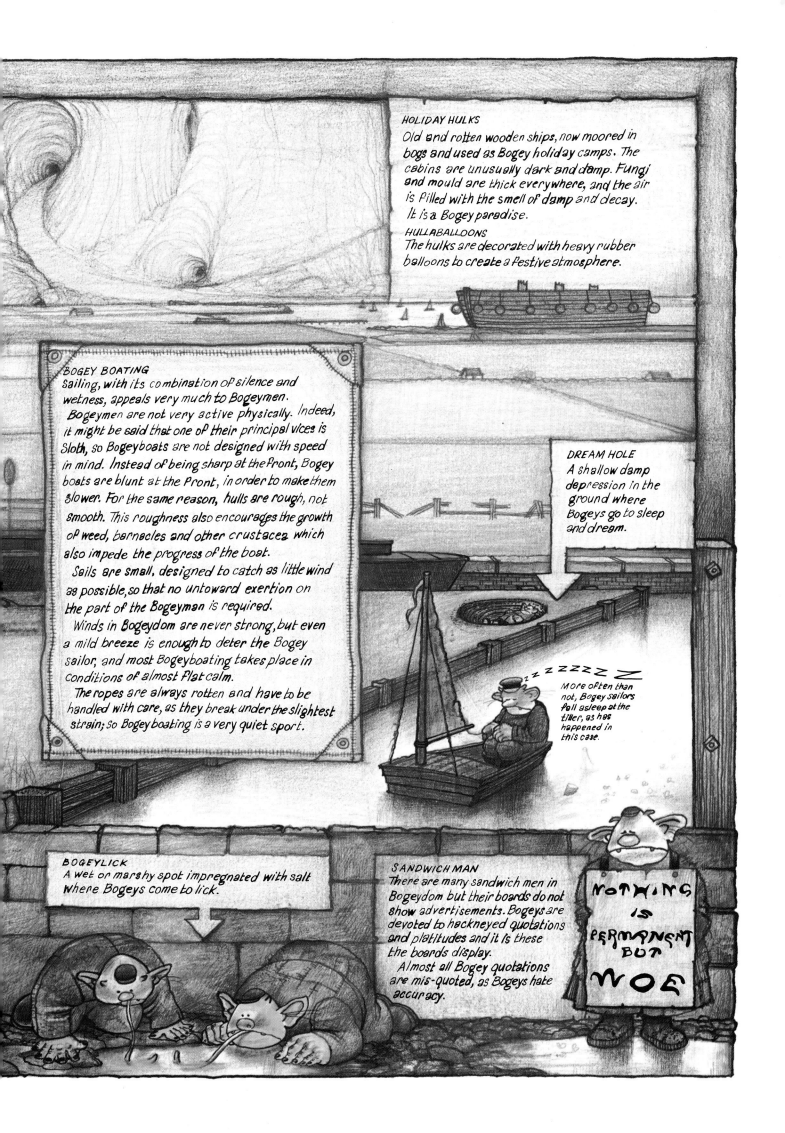

HOLIDAY HULKS
Old and rotten wooden ships, now moored in bogs and used as Bogey holiday camps. The cabins are unusually dark and damp. Fungi and mould are thick everywhere, and the air is filled with the smell of damp and decay. It is a Bogey paradise.

HULLABALLOONS
The hulks are decorated with heavy rubber balloons to create a festive atmosphere.

BOGEY BOATING
Sailing, with its combination of silence and wetness, appeals very much to Bogeymen.

Bogeymen are not very active physically. Indeed, it might be said that one of their principal vices is Sloth, so Bogeyboats are not designed with speed in mind. Instead of being sharp at the front, Bogey boats are blunt at the front, in order to make them slower. For the same reason, hulls are rough, not smooth. This roughness also encourages the growth of weed, barnacles and other crustacea which also impede the progress of the boat.

Sails are small, designed to catch as little wind as possible, so that no untoward exertion on the part of the Bogeyman is required.

Winds in Bogeydom are never strong, but even a mild breeze is enough to deter the Bogey sailor, and most Bogeyboating takes place in conditions of almost flat calm.

The ropes are always rotten and have to be handled with care, as they break under the slightest strain; so Bogeyboating is a very quiet sport.

DREAM HOLE
A shallow damp depression in the ground where Bogeys go to sleep and dream.

ZZZZZZZ Z
More often than not, Bogey sailors fall asleep at the tiller, as has happened in this case.

BOGEYLICK
A wet or marshy spot impregnated with salt where Bogeys come to lick.

SANDWICH MAN
There are many sandwich men in Bogeydom but their boards do not show advertisements. Bogeys are devoted to hackneyed quotations and platitudes and it is these the boards display.

Almost all Bogey quotations are mis-quoted, as Bogeys hate accuracy.

NOTHING IS PERMANENT BUT WOE

ODEUM

A large, cinema-like building where Bogies go to enjoy Smells and Odours. Here, they also listen to whispered poems about Smells, known as Odes. Odalisques are in attendance; these are young Bogey ladies in saucy pill-box hats, with straps under the chin, flowing capes and wide trousers.

The performance begins when the oditorium is darkened and a glowing Odour Organ rises majestically from beneath the floor. Then, as the Organist skilfully operates the controls appalling smells are wafted over the audience.

These are greeted with rapturous "Ooohs!" and "Aaaahs!" similar to the sounds made at Surface firework displays. "Oh, odious! Odious!" come the ecstatic cries after a particularly fine smell.

Later, odists come on stage and whisper their odes, but this is a very secondary part of the entertainment. Despite their much-vaunted love of literature, Bogeys are sensuous rather than intellectual, and the Smells always come first.

O DEUM

GONE WITH THE WI

SMELLING TONIGHT

PICNIC AREA

A steam of rich distill'd perfumes.

BOGEY BOYS ABDICATE OK

An amazing Stereobogoleograph of an Odalisque

I am a man of unclean lips and I dwell in the midst of a people of unclean lips.....

PIG-STICKING

An ancient sport in Bogeydom.

The basis of the sport is extremely simple. Each competitor has a pig which he sticks to the wall with Muck. The last pig to fall to the ground is the winner. The pigs have only a few inches to fall, so no injury results. Baby pigs are usually preferred, as they are lighter in weight, but some expert pig-stickers prefer old sows as they do not wriggle so much.

Due to the improvement in the quality of Muck over the years, these competitions can last for hours, or even days, and the pigs have to be fed and watered whilst stuck to the wall.

The Bogeys sleep through the contest if it lasts more than a few hours.

APPLAUD US WHEN WE STICK
CONSOLE US WHEN WE FALL

Foulest Quality MAGIMUCK BRILLIANT BROWN Satin Finish Contains POLYURITHANE

YE OLDE BOGEY BATTERYES

These ancient structures are found near the borders of Bogeydom, and were made for defence against Napoleybogey.

The walls of the batteries were built of soggy Muck to make them difficult for the enemy to climb. The Quaker Guns * at the top were calculated to inspire fear in the hearts of the enemy when viewed from a distance. (All Bogey guns are made of wood. They make no noise, have no ammunition, and do not fire. Long ago, Bogeys realised that metal guns did far more harm than good, so wooden ones were introduced. These have been found to be much more satisfactory, as they are silent and harmless.)

However, the wooden guns were so rotten, they fell to pieces when ever they were moved. The dummy wooden cannon balls were used by the gunners for playing bowels (Bogey bowls) though they were of little use even for this purpose, because they were Bogey balls and therefore not round and consequently rolled about in a promiscuous fashion.

As the Bogeys had no idea from which direction Napoleybogey would come, the Quaker Guns were, of course, quaquaversal.

* QUAKER GUN: a wooden gun mounted to deceive the enemy.

POSTERS

Bogey posters do not advertise coming events; they advertise past events. By the time a Bogey sees the poster, the event which it announces has long since passed. Consequently, he does not need to write down times and dates, book tickets or travel, and can thus proceed with his normal indolent life in peace.

TIDDLYWINKS

Bogeymen are devoted to the game of Tiddlywinks, probably because it is silent and requires no exertion. As with most Bogey games, the object is to achieve a draw. This is not difficult, as Bogey tiddlywinks are made, not of bone, but of dried Muck. As a result, they usually snap in two when pressed one against the other and in damp weather they become soggy and useless.

The pot into which the tiddlywinks are aimed is filled with dirty water and if, by any chance a tiddlywink should fall into the pot, it instantly dissolves.

BOGEY ANGLING

This is another very popular Bogey sport.

Its popularity again may be due to its quietness and lack of movement. To make the sport even less energetic, the main aim of Bogey angling is to avoid catching fish.

Bogeymen dislike the fuss and bother of having to land a fish once hooked. Another aspect they dislike is having to disgorge the hook from the struggling creature's mouth. Bogeymen are extremely gentle and sensitive by nature (when not at work) and the anguished process of removing a hook from a fish's mouth will always reduce them to tears.

It is an unwritten law of Bogey angling, that, having once caught a fish, the Bogey angler leaves the waterside at once and goes shamefacedly home, not to return that day.

The same evening, sympathetic companions will buy him a pot of slime in a Bogeybar and try to alleviate his sense of guilt and failure.

BOGEY TACKLE

Bogey fishing tackle, like everything else in Bogeydom, is old, rotten and decayed. Bogeymen hate newness and efficiency.

So, in their form of angling, where the main aim is to avoid catching fish the worse the state of the tackle, the better the chance of catching nothing.

Rods are made of old and rotting wood, lines are knotted, mouldy and ancient, floats are water-logged and hooks are rusty and blunt. Consequently, even if a fish is hooked, with this tackle it is almost impossible to land it. The line will break, the hook will bend, or the rod will snap and the fish will get away.

BOGEYFISH

Bogeyfish themselves are even more indolent than the anglers who try not to catch them. They live on the muddy bottoms of the canals and are very inert. Half buried in mud and surrounded by rubbish, they rarely move so require little food. The Bogey anglers' hooks drift harmlessly by above their heads and the somnolent Bogeyfish rarely notice them

So neither fish nor angler have much to do with one another, and each can lead his separate life in peace.

BOGEY BITTERNS

Here in the Upper Tunnels can be heard the hollow booming call of the Bogey Bitterns. These flightless birds stalk in the shadows on their long pale legs and are rarely seen, even by Bogeymen.

Like Surface Bitterns, and like Bogeymen themselves, they are SOLITARY, SKULKING, and CREPUSCULAR.

HE PLUNGES HOUSES INTO DARKNESS

I wonder if it does *them* any good?

OH DAMN! THAT'S A FUSE GONE!

WHERE'S THE TORCH?

WHO'S MOVED THE MATCHES?

WUFF! WUFF!

MUM!

OUCH! MY HEAD!

HE TAPS AT WINDOWS.....

I can't think what else I could do..

I MUST CUT THAT TREE. THE TWIGS ARE TAPPING ON THE GLASS.

I'VE TOLD YOU ABOUT IT OFTEN ENOUGH.

Almost all Bogeys carry a big stick.
   The sticks are used for testing the depth of mire, for poking people in bed, and for many other un-mentionable Bogey practices. They are made of bog oak and are extremely smelly.
   Bogeys also use their sticks as comforters, and in moments of anxiety or loneliness, the stick is fondled and even cuddled. The lonely Bogey is often seen sucking the stick for the bog juices it contains, and sniffing its bog odours, which remind him of home far below.

HE MAKES "THINGS THAT GO BUMP IN THE NIGHT."

I used to think it fun when I was younger...

BUMP!

WHATEVER'S THAT? IT WOKE ME UP.

DON'T BE FRIGHTENED, DEAR I'M HERE

HE TURNS DOOR KNOBS VERY, VERY SLOWLY...

I used to enjoy it...

WHAT'S THAT? OH MY GOLLY! THE KNOBS TURNING! GO AWAY! HELP!

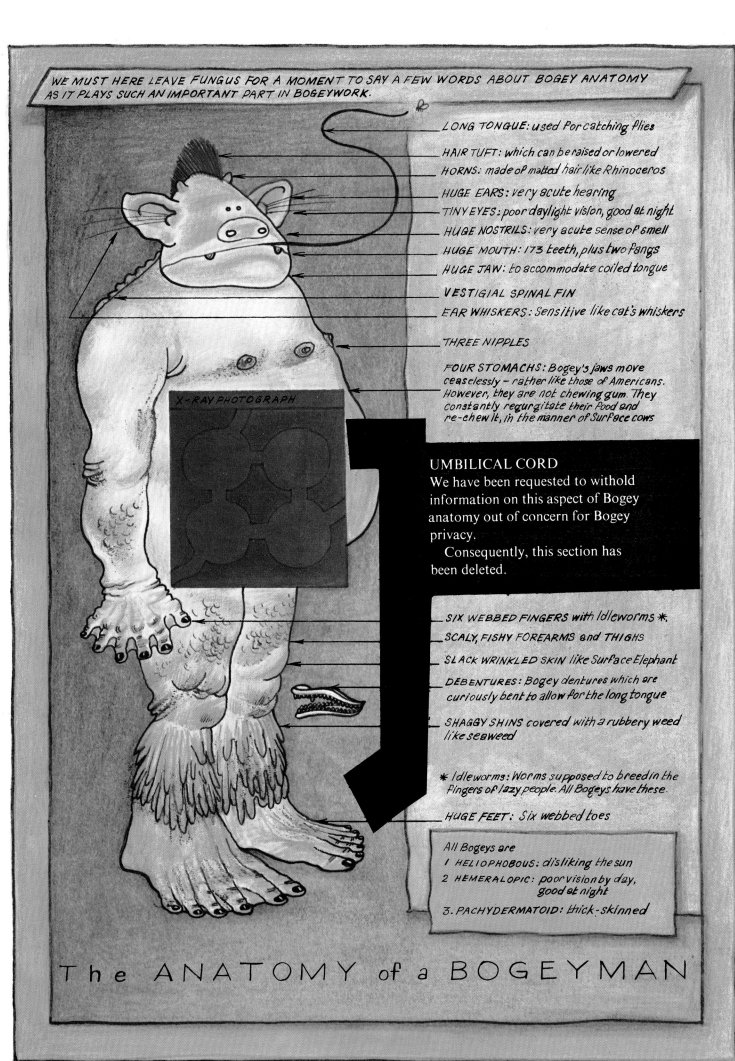

The ANATOMY of a BOGEYMAN

Bogey anatomy is adapted to wetness and cold. To survive in the dryness and warmth of The Surface, Bogeymen occasionally need special CLOTHING and EQUIPMENT

KONISCOPE: An instrument for indicating the amount of dust in the atmosphere. Bogeymen are allergic to dust, pollen and all other manifestations of dryness

LAMBREQUIN or HAVELOCK: a light covering worn over the head and neck as a protection against moonstroke

STERCORACEOUS * DUNGAREES

DROSOMETER: An instrument for measuring the quantity of dew falling on a body during the night

KEELIVINES: Lead-pencils

IMPERMEATOR: a contrivance for lubricating the interior surfaces of a Bogeyman's trousers by the pumping in of oily slime

DASYMETER: an instrument for measuring the density of gases (or smells)

LAMBOYS: A kilted skirt of rusty metal plates, now very old-fashioned and worn only by elderly Bogeymen. Its purpose is to direct valuable evaporations which may have escaped the gennets (q.v.) back to the Bogeyman's vital parts

FOGLE: handkerchief: Bogeymen retain the English 18th century term for these — MUCKENDER

GENICULATES: Bogey knee-bags, popularly known as GENNETS. These protect the knees (as Bogeywork entails a hantle * of kneeling and crawling), but their main purpose is to seal off the boot tops and prevent the evaporation of precious fluids and smells. They also help to prevent GONAGRA (gout in the knee). GENIPAP is the name given to the muck found in the gennets after a night's work. It has an orange colour and a vinous taste

* STERCORACEOUS: pertaining to, or composed of dung

* hantle: a good deal

It sometimes happens that a Bogeyman finds himself unable to reach a Bogeyhole before daylight. If he cannot find a cool, dark hiding place, he will bury himself in a shady spot. In this manner he will evade the heat of the sun and preserve his vital wetness. He will then sleep till darkness falls again.

It is during this time that his projecting hair tuft and ears are sometimes mistaken for a plant. This "plant" was said by the ancients to have a root resembling the human form and to shriek when pulled up; and it is this that lies behind the legend of the Mandragora or MANDRAKE.

HE PEERS INTO LIGHTED WINDOWS.....

It's just a routine now..

AAAAIIIIEEEE

HE BANGS DOORS.....

OH LORD! I COULD HAVE SWORN I LOCKED UP!

BANG! BANG! BANG!

Will Mould just go on doing the same thing?

FUNGUS TAKES A FEW WRIGGLING THINGS FROM HIS BOGEYBAG AND DROPS THEM THROUGH THE LETTER BOX...

HE RUMMAGES THROUGH DUSTBINS FOR TASTY SCRAN * TO TAKE HOME, AND MAKES AS MUCH NOISE AS POSSIBLE

BANG!

BLESSED CATS ARE AT THE BINS AGAIN!

I KNOW— WOKE ME UP.

CLANG!

* SCRAN: Broken victuals; scraps, refuse

HE KNOCKS SLATES OFF ROOFS.....

I'm quite happy, really. It's just that I'd like to know WHY...

OH DAMN! THERE GOES ANOTHER SLATE!

HE SENDS SOOT DOWN CHIMNEYS.....

There's the Camera Club, and my boat and the garden, and my photo album....

OH! AAARGH!

UGH! AARGH!

FUNGUS PASSES AN INTEREST

Photography class in the evening...

MURK QUINSY · FLABBER SQUINSY · QUEINMY

INTERSECT: A species of Bogey Fly which inhabits the Interests and causes a degree of nuisance by laying its eggs in the sleepers' nostrils. Few Bogeys seem to object, however, and on awakening merely sniff up the maggots like snuff, or blow them downwards onto their tongue and eat them.

INTERESTS

There are many Interests in Bogeydom. It is here that Bogeys go whenever they are tired, bored or oppressed by worries. They are then interred by the Interns and sleep for as long as they like, (up to a limit of one year.) No one, not even a close relation, is allowed to waken them for any reason whatsoever. Many painful problems are avoided in this manner and it may account for Bogey longevity. When the sleeper awakes, the problem has receded so far into the past it might never have existed at all.

A one year limit was set as it was found that a longer period caused psychological and social problems of re-adjustment. After two or more years some dis-orientation was observed.

Bogeys can live off the fat of their bodies in the same way as hibernating Surface animals. Apart from a sprinkling of water in dry weather, the sleepers require no attention at all.

The crosses are simply labels with the Bogey's name and date for awakening.

BOGEY PHOTOGRAPHY

It is surprising how many Bogeys are keen photographers in view of the darkness and dirt of the Bogey world. Photography is an art which demands light and cleanliness, perhaps more than any other.

However, Bogeymen are to be seen everywhere with their waterproof cameras, which have huge lenses to cope with the inadequate light of Bogeydom.

The results, judged by Surface standards, are not inspiring. The Bogey's lens is usually filthy, and the film has been put in with twelve dirty, sticky fingers.

The laboratories at BOGAK are choked with dirt and slime, and the films are often mouldy before the Bogey buys them.

The resulting prints, dark to the point of impenetrability, scratched, dirty and mouldy are regarded by Bogeymen with pride and delight.

They are stuck in mildewy albums and proudly shown to visitors.

Here we see an unusually fine example of a Bogachome print (19 secs. at f 1·8)

Not to reason why.... not ask questions... just keep bogling away... frightening Drycleaners, ✻ drinking slime... taking photographs.... reading about the history of Muck.... best not to think about what it's all FOR...

✻ Drycleaners: the Surface people

THE NATIONAL BOGEY GALLERY

Perhaps because there is virtually no music in the Bogey world, Bogeys are all the more devoted to the art of Painting. This is possibly because of its Silence, though an added attraction may be that paintings can be dirty. Bogeys like their paintings to be filthy, and contained in filthy frames.

On Sunday afternoons, the National Bogey Gallery is a popular place. Its lugubrious halls are filled with troops of families, quietly squelching round on the wet marble floors in their Bogeyboots and soggy coats. The air is filled with quiet hisses of admiration.

Water drips from the high arched ceilings and dim lights shine over the dismal rhyparographs.*

The pictures are thickly coated with sticky non-drying varnish to make them waterproof and to collect more dirt.

Still-lifes show bowls of rotting fruit and vases of dead flowers. Landscapes show ditches, dead trees, sewer out flows and black stagnant lakes. In animal paintings the subjects are usually dead. Figure paintings depict sad and often sentimental scenes.

But sometimes, despite the sentimentality, these paintings are quite touching. They are often about Love, mostly Forlorn or Hopeless Love, or about Death – particularly the death of Bogey babies.

Bogey families are often to be seen in tears in front of these pictures.

*rhyparographs: paintings of mean or sordid subjects

BV or BOGEYVISION

Bogey Television, like Bogey Radio, is almost silent. Bogeys have extremely sensitive hearing and their television speaks in a whisper, and of course, has no music.

Programmes are on the usual Bogey interests – Filth and Muck, or Gloom, Despondency and Dark, but occasionally, late at night, when the Bogey babies are safely in bed, Horror films are shown of Sunlight, flowers, cornfields and hot dry beaches with Drycleaners laughing gaily and playing loud music.

These films have recently become a somewhat perverse cult in the Bogey world, popular with a certain section of the Young Bogeys.

These "drop-ins" also profess to like bright colours and noise. Ancient gramophone recordings and abandoned equipment have been smuggled in from Surface rubbish dumps and these are used with a total disregard for tradition, custom, and even law. Worse still, some of the more extreme members of the cult began keeping themselves clean, scraping off their protective layers of dirt and slime and taking baths in warm, clean water.

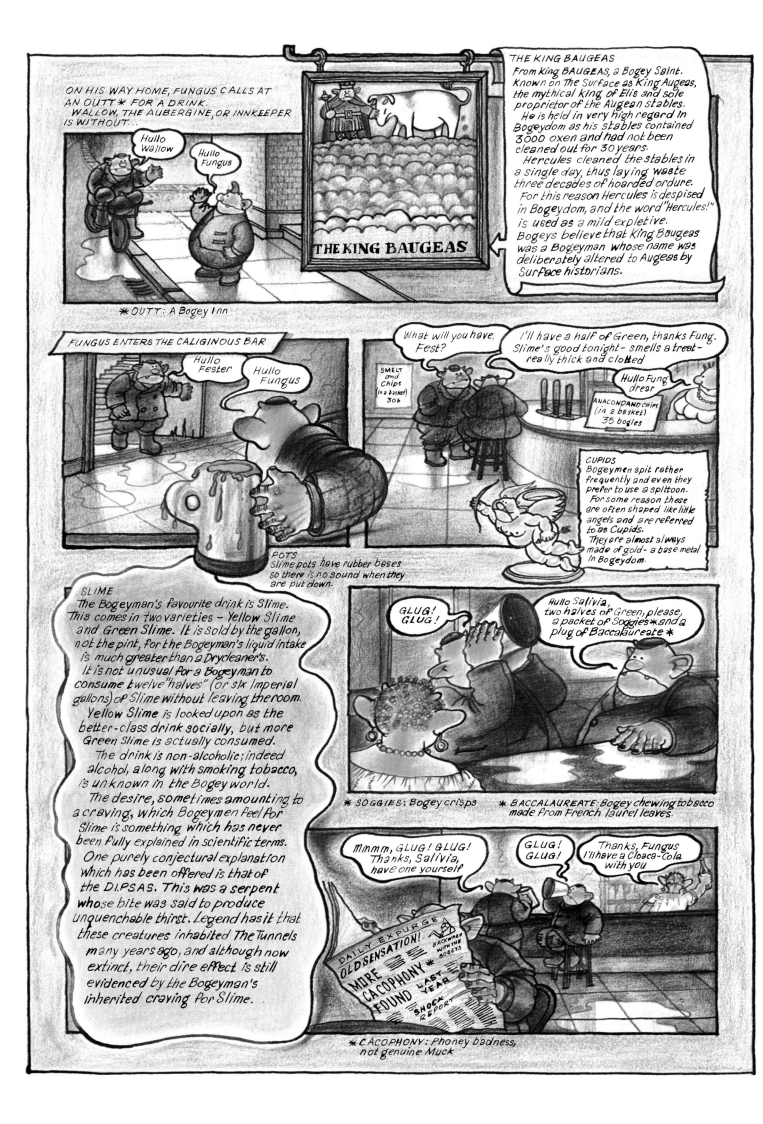

ON HIS WAY HOME, FUNGUS CALLS AT AN OUTT✲ FOR A DRINK. WALLOW, THE AUBERGINE, OR INNKEEPER IS WITHOUT...

Hullo Wallow

Hullo Fungus

THE KING BAUGEAS

✲ OUTT: A Bogey Inn

THE KING BAUGEAS
From King BAUGEAS, a Bogey Saint. Known on The Surface as King Augeas, the mythical king of Elis and sole proprietor of the Augean stables.
He is held in very high regard in Bogeydom as his stables contained 3,000 oxen and had not been cleaned out for 30 years.
Hercules cleaned the stables in a single day, thus laying waste three decades of hoarded ordure.
For this reason Hercules is despised in Bogeydom, and the word "Hercules!" is used as a mild expletive.
Bogeys believe that King Baugeas was a Bogeyman whose name was deliberately altered to Augeas by Surface historians.

FUNGUS ENTERS THE CALIGINOUS BAR

Hullo Fester

Hullo Fungus

What will you have, Fest?

I'll have a half of Green, thanks Fung. Slime's good tonight— smells a treat— really thick and clotted

SMELT and Chips (in a basket) 30b

Hullo Fung dear

ANACONDAND CHIPS (in a basket) 35 bogles

CUPIDS
Bogeymen spit rather frequently and even they prefer to use a spittoon.
For some reason these are often shaped like little angels and are referred to as Cupids.
They are almost always made of gold— a base metal in Bogeydom.

POTS
Slime pots have rubber bases so there is no sound when they are put down.

SLIME
The Bogeyman's favourite drink is Slime. This comes in two varieties — Yellow Slime and Green Slime. It is sold by the gallon, not the pint, for the Bogeyman's liquid intake is much greater than a Drycleaner's.
It is not unusual for a Bogeyman to consume twelve "halves" (or six Imperial gallons) of Slime without leaving the room.
Yellow Slime is looked upon as the better-class drink socially, but more Green Slime is actually consumed.
The drink is non-alcoholic; indeed alcohol, along with smoking tobacco, is unknown in the Bogey world.
The desire, sometimes amounting to a craving, which Bogeymen feel for Slime is something which has never been fully explained in scientific terms.
One purely conjectural explanation which has been offered is that of the D.I.P.S.A.S. This was a serpent whose bite was said to produce unquenchable thirst. Legend has it that these creatures inhabited The Tunnels many years ago, and although now extinct, their dire effect is still evidenced by the Bogeyman's inherited craving for Slime.

GLUG! GLUG!

Hullo Salivia, two halves of Green, please, a packet of Soggies✲ and a plug of Baccalaureate✲

✲ SOGGIES: Bogey crisps

✲ BACCALAUREATE: Bogey chewing tobacco made from French laurel leaves.

Mmmm, GLUG! GLUG! Thanks, Salivia, have one yourself

GLUG! GLUG!

Thanks, Fungus I'll have a Cloaca-Cola with you

DAILY EXPURGE
OLD SENSATION!
BACKWARD WITH THE BOGEYS
MORE CACOPHONY✲ FOUND LAST YEAR
SHOCK REPORT

✲ CACOPHONY: Phoney badness, not genuine Muck

MUSIC
Although there is no background music in Bogeybars, there is often a recording playing of favourite Bogey sounds.
These usually consist of running sewer water, the drip of slime in echoing cellars, and the moaning of chill winds in lonely tunnels.
This is music to the sensitive ears of Bogeymen.

You seem a bit fed up, Fungus

Umm - Well - GLUG! GLUG! Sometimes I wonder what it's all about...

BOGEY DARTS
The object of Bogey darts is to miss the board. Hitting the board counts as a "miss" and is scored against the thrower. Hitting the wall counts as a "cow," (or bull) and scores 0. As it is fairly easy to miss the board there is rarely any score.
For quietness Bogey darts have rubber suckers instead of metal points.

What what's about? GLUG! GLUG! Oooh! It's nice the way the slime slips down

US. What are we FOR?

FOR???

Yes. Why are you a Bogeyman?

BOGEY BILLIARDS
Here again, the object of the game is to avoid getting the balls into the holes. This is not difficult as the balls are slightly larger than the holes and so cannot go in. The cues are worm-eaten and often snap in the middle of a game.
The bed of the table is made of a slab of pressed Muck called Bogiboard. This is highly absorbent and soon becomes soggy in the damp atmosphere. It then produces the humps, hollows and even puddles which characterise the true Bogey billiards table.

CESS: A variety of Bogey water cress grown in cess pools.

CESS 2 BOGLES

Why am I? Well! What else would I be?

You might be a Drycleaner

STERCORAREUS CREPIDATUS "DIRTY ALLAN"
A Surface seabird, much admired in Bogeydom for its habit of devouring the regurgitated food which it has forced other birds to disgorge.

What! ME?? Not likely! Catch me up there! All hot and dry! Stinking flowers everywhere LIGHT! WARMTH! SUN! - No fear.....

But if you were a DC you'd like all that...

Yes, but I'm not! I'm a Bogey and proud of it!

But what are we pestering and frightening them FOR?

FOR? Why ask what for? You might as well ask what Slime's for. GLUG! GLUG! GLUG! Come on and have another and forget it.

SO, AFTER ANOTHER HALF OF SLIME FUNGUS BIDS HIS COMPANIONS BOIBYE AND BOGLES HIS WAY THROUGH THE MIRE TO THE PUBLIC LIBERALITY.....

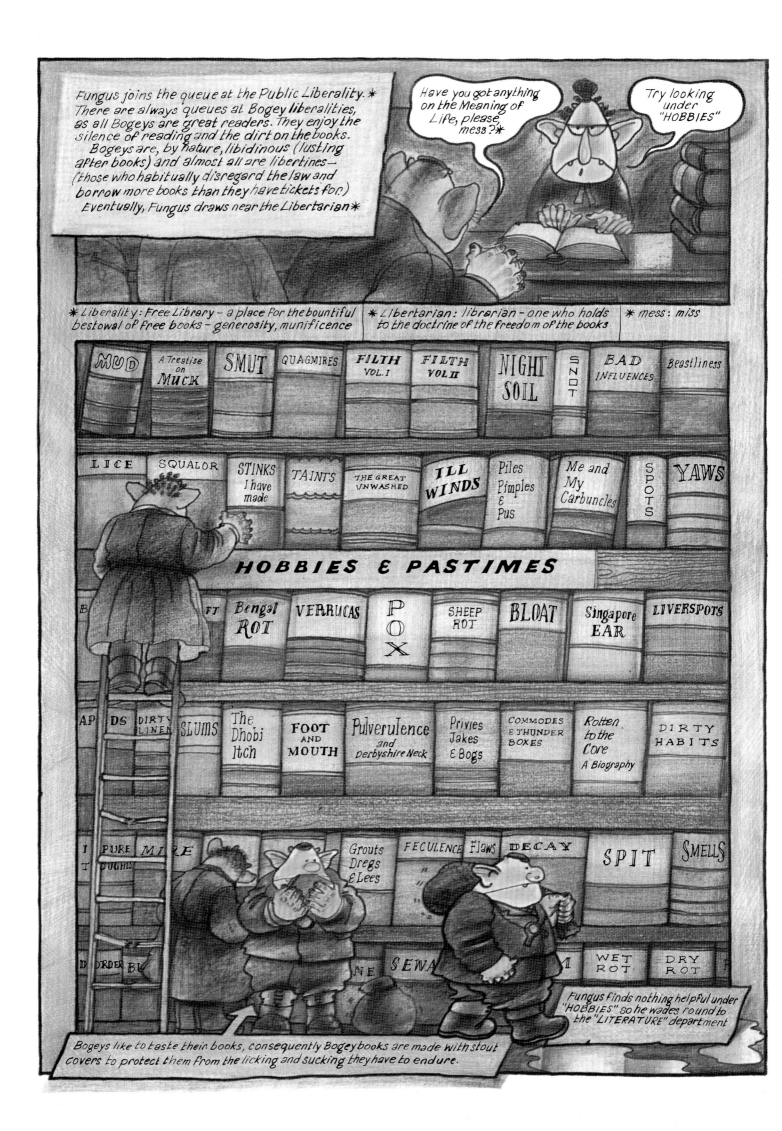

It must be pointed out, regrettably, that there is very little original Bogey literature.

Bogeys have very small tops to their heads; consequently, their brains are too small for the production of great literary works, such as this book you are reading.

Most Bogey books are taken from The Surface and are selected for their closeness to Bogey thought and feeling, or somewhat crudely adapted to fit Bogey themes.

This sad fact is never acknowledged by Bogeys. Over the years they seem to have successfully repressed all memory of it, and now genuinely believe their literature to have been entirely created by Bogeys.

(The pages of Bogey books are made of plastic to withstand the damp of the Bogey world. This is why they are so thick.)

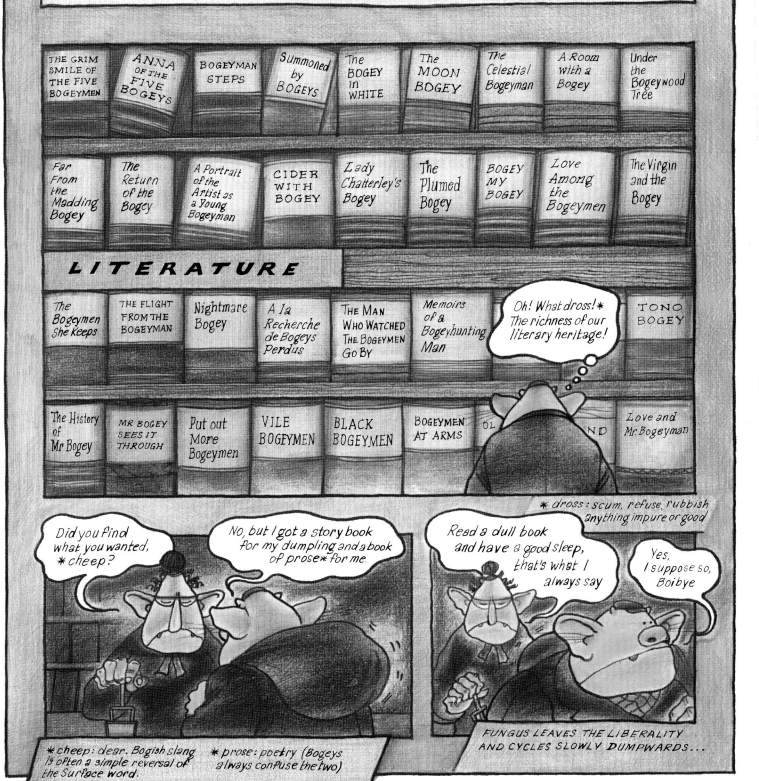

FUNGUS LEAVES THE LIBERALITY AND CYCLES SLOWLY DUMPWARDS...

Before going indoors Fungus has a look at his garden....

Hmmm.... This new rose is a bit gemmiparous...

* gemmiparous: producing buds

Hullo Mucus, Hullo Pus

BOGEY PETS
CATS: The Bogey cat has evolved into a hairless creature with a green frog-like skin. Normal cat fur was useless in the wet Bogey conditions.

DOGS: Bogeys gave up having dogs centuries ago, when they realised how noisy and clean they were. Skunks were then introduced and have since become universally popular and hairless.

BOGEY GARDENING or DWINING ✶
Bogey gardening is a strange art.
Bogeys do not like flowers. They hate their bright colours and sweet scent. They love the fading greens and pale yellows of dying leaves. They love the smell of decay.
So the whole art of Bogey gardening is to make the plants slowly fade and die. If a flower blooms a Bogey gardener feels he has failed. Blooms in a Bogey garden are the sign of a lazy gardener, as weeds are in Surface gardens.
✶ DWINING : causing to waste or pine away

Mmmm..... really marcescent ✶

So melts, so vanisheth, so fades, so withers...

The dwine is doing very well. Fungus is proud of it. Everything is dying nicely. There is not a bloom to be seen. The air is full of the scent of decay. The acid soil smells, the rotting vegetation smells. It is a real Bogey dwine.

✶ marcescent: withering without falling

① **BOGEY FLAGS**
Bogeymen are patriotic and many of them fly the national flag. This has no design or colours and is a plain muddy brown – symbolic of Muck, the Bogey Staff of Life. Bogeys cannot bear the fissling ✶ of flags, so their flags are made of stone.
These are known as flag stones.

② **MOSS BUNKER or WEEM ✶**
Almost all Bogey gardens contain a Moss Bunker. They are situated in the dampest part of the garden and are covered with moss. Inside there is always at least six binches of slimy water and the walls and ceilings are covered with fungi.
These bunkers are used as shelters in periods of dry weather, when the house becomes uncomfortably dry and itchy. Drainage kennels, or channels, carry water from outside into the bunker.
Two or three taps are fitted and there is often an emergency water supply on the roof.

③ **BOGLET**
A small decorative bog as in a Bogey suburban dwine.

✶ fissling: rustling
✶ WEEM: a subterranean chamber lined with rough stones

④ **BORDURE**
A border composed of ordure.

⑤ **QUOITS**
A popular Bogey garden game.
The quoits or rings are thrown at a Quoin. The lack of competitiveness in Bogeys is clearly shown in this game. The quoins are far too big to be ringed by the quoits so no one can win and the game can go on for hours or even days.
Wooden quoins are preferred to stone as stone never goes rotten. The disadvantage of a wooden quoin is that it wears thin over the years and sometimes becomes so reduced that a ring will fall over it. It then has to be replaced.

⑥ **HODDEN**
A midden full of hodmandods.

OOOPS!

* INDUVIAE: the withered remains of leaves which remain and decay on the stems of plants

ICTERUS

A disease of plants causing yellowing of the leaves and consequently much encouraged in Bogey gardens.

ICTERUS is also the name of a Bogey mythological hero. The story is similar to the Greek legend of Icarus, and it is no doubt popular because it embodies the Bogey dislike of technology, sunlight and heat.

The symbolic fall, away from sunlight and heat, downwards, into the cold darkness of the ocean, is seen with great sympathy and approval by Bogeys.

In the Bogey legend, Icterus does not perish in the sea, but plunges through the soft mire of the ocean bed until he emerges in a Bogeyhole. He then returns to Bogeydom, covered in cold, wet Muck and purged of his perverse desires for light, heat and height.

Unfortunately, he had flown too near the sun and his natural green colour had been bleached away. He returned to Bogeydom a ghastly yellow and was known ever after as ICTERUS (Greek, IKTEROS : Jaundice)

Put your clothes in to soak or they'll be all dry in the morning — there's a good boy

Can I have a gumboil * Mum?

Not when you've just blackened your teeth!

* INJELLY: imbed in jelly. Bogey babies sleep in a tin of cold jelly

* gumboils: Bogey sweets

There's a big slug for you — it'll keep you nice and cool. Try not to throw your blunket * off, drear

There's a pot of cold slime by the bed. Don't forget to pour it over yourself if you get dry in the night. Daddy will be up in a minute......

*blunket: a blanket soaked in sour junket, used on Bogey babies' beds

(1) THE MAN IN THE MOON

For centuries Bogeys have believed that the Man in the Moon was a Bogeyman. Surface scholars have always dismissed this idea, but it must be admitted that there is considerable evidence in its favour.

> The man in the moon
> Came down too soon
> And asked his way to Norwich
> He went by the south,
> And burnt his mouth
> With supping on cold plum porridge.

If it is assumed that the Man in the Moon was a Bogeyman, the logic behind this apparent nonsense at once becomes clear.

1 "Came down too soon": too early (i.e.) before dawn. After the brightness of the moon his sensitive Bogey eyes would be unaccustomed to the blackness of night on Earth. He should have waited for the gentle light of dawn, similar in intensity to moonlight. However, he blunders about, lost in the darkness, and finally asks the way to Norwich, knowing it to be a district particularly rich in Bogey holes.

2. "He went by the south"

A Bogeyman would always go by the south, to avail himself of the moist south-westerly winds. The north would be colder, but also drier. The Bogeyman's need for wetness is always greater than his need for cold.

3. "Norwich"

Nor-ridge: (i.e.) North Ridge. A ridge giving protection from the drying north-easterly winds and producing a damp south-west-facing slope ideal for Bogeyholes. This is why so many are found in the district.

4. "plum porridge"

If a Bogey moon man returned to Earth he would obviously come in winter. After the coldness of outer space, even winter temperatures would seem warm to a Bogeyman. So he came in mid-winter soon after Christmas day. The availability of cold plum porridge (i.e. plum pudding or Christmas pudding) indicates the time of year fairly accurately.

5. "burnt his mouth"

Who but a Bogeyman could burn his mouth on cold plum porridge?

(2) BOGEYBEAR

The toy replica of the adults' Bugbear. Many Bogey houses and all Bogey bloaters* keep a Bugbear. The filthy fur of these small somnolent bears is infested with a species of bug which Bogies find particularly delicious.

* bloaters: restaurants

(3) HUMPTY BOGGART *

Humpty Boggart, known to the Surface as Humphrey Bogart, is one of the few drycleaners popular in Bogeydom. To Bogey children he is a folk hero and his wicked ways are greatly admired. It is generally believed that he was a Bogeyman whose name was altered on the Surface to conceal his true origins.

* BOGGART: Northern English; Bogey, Bogle, Hobgoblin

TURDUS
(TURDIDAE)

The Man in the Moon

A is for APPLE

B is for BOG

C is for COWPAT

E is for EEL

F is for FLOWER

M is for MOUSE

O is for ORANGE

P is for PIMPLES

S is for STAIN

T is for TADPOLE TART

U is for * UMBRELLA

LT | REWARDS AND BOGEYS | Anne OF GREEN BOGEYS | The Fifth Form at St. Bogeynicks | TOM'S MIDNIGHT BOGEY | My Naughty Little Bogey | The Tale of the FLOPSY BOGIES | The Little Grey Bogies | A CHILD'S GARDEN OF BOGEYS | BOGGLES FLIES NORTH | The Tale OF BENJAMIN BOGEY | CHARLIE AND THE CHOCOLATE BOGIES

6 Bogey umbrellas are upside-down. They are designed to catch water and shower it onto the user.

4 TURDUS
A genus of passerine birds of the family TURDIDAE, comprising the Thrush, Blackbird, Ring Ouzel, Redwing and Fieldfare.
  One of the few varieties of Surface birds in which Bogeys show any interest.

5 BOGGIEWOGS
The Bogey Golliwog. These are a caricature of pink Drycleaners. They always have huge blue eyes, rosebud mouths and curly blond hair.

Every night Fungus reads to Mould from the BIG BOGEYOLOGY BOOK. Every Bogeyman possesses one of these stupendous volumes – it is the Bogey Bible. In its plastic pages is described the whole art of the Bogeyman – "THE WORK", as it is reverently known.
  By these nightly readings, Fungus introduces his son to the arcane mysteries of Bogeywork.
  Overleaf, you are privileged to be shown four pages from this wondrous tome.

ELEMENTARY BOGEYOLOGY: Contents

 How to make Beds feel Lumpy.

 How to make Bottom Sheets Ruck-Up round the Feet.

 One hundred ways to hide a sock so the DC can find only one in the morning

 Fifty tricks to play with Alarm Clocks

WHAT HAS THE NIGHT

ELEMENTARY BOGEYOLOGY: Contents

WEIGHT OF BOGEY BAG OVER LEFT BOOT
RIGHT BOGEY BOOT RAISED
WEIGHT OVER LEFT BOGEY BOOT

CREAK!

Ten different ways of making Creepy Creaks on Stairs

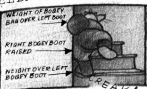 How to LURK, Including LOITERING WITH INTENT, SKULKING, and HOW TO LIE IN WAIT

 How to make GURGLES IN CISTERNS and HISSINGS IN PIPES including The Art of the Ball-Cock

THE ART OF THE BOGEYBAG

TO DO WITH SLEEP?...

ADVANCED BOGEYOLOGY: Contents

 The Use of the Tongue in the Application of Slime

 The Use of the Bogey Stick

◁ NB. Note large dollop OF MUCK

ADVANCED BOGEYOLOGY: Contents

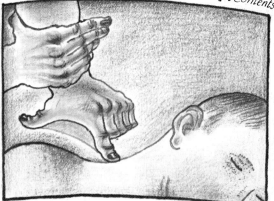

THE CREATION OF BOILS

This, the Supreme Achievevement of the Bogeyman's Art, borders on the Magical.

It is not a charm vouchsafed to every Bogeyman. It is an art that demands an inborn gift, great concentration and long practice.

Then, by merely pressing a finger on the neck of the sleeping DC, a boil can be engendered.

Soon, it will begin to swell, and in the fullness of time, when it reaches maturity, it will flower forth and then, the glorious golden pus

Another volume of importance to Bogeys is shown here. This is the Field Guide, and it is used by Bogey Cubs and Bogey Brownies. These children are far too young to take up mature Bogey work, but Nature Rambles Up Top and the study of Drycleaners introduces them to the Surface World and teaches them Field Craft, Silence, Concealment and many other Bogey skills.

"Now son, we come to window rattling...."

"Dear little Mould....
Thou still unravish'd
Boy of Quietness
Thou foster child of Silence and
Slow Time....."

Where to Watch DRYCLEANERS

A Field Guide to Surface Life

A PINK   A BROWN

Precise Field Identification of every Species of Drycleaner occurring on The Surface

1200 ILLUSTRATIONS · 650 IN COLOUR

With an INTRODUCTION BY SIR JULIAN BOGEY

WHERE TO WATCH DRYCLEANERS

Drycleaners live on The Surface. There are three main species of Drycleaner – the Pinks, the Browns, and the Yellows. There are no Green Drycleaners.

LESSER YELLOW DRYCLEANER (Immature Male)

LESSER SPOTTED PINK DRYCLEANER (Immature Male)

LESSER BROWN DRYCLEANER (Immature Female)

Drycleaners have no horns or fins. They are dry in texture with very little body slime. They smell only faintly, though occasionally a good stench will be found emanating from the ███████ or, in hot weather, from the ███ and the ███

The words deleted on this page were considered offensive and unsuitable for Surface publication.

WHERE TO WATCH DRYCLEANERS

PINKS: (Pinkornithidae)

Identification: 60"–76"
Resemble very large Bogeys but with brilliant pink skin. Huge-topped heads with dense growth of hair all over. Tiny, malformed ears and tiny noses (poor hearing, poor sense of smell.) Minute mouths with thick pink lips. No umbilical cord. Only five fingers.
   Adult males have hair growth on lower part of face. Adult females have only TWO chest bumps.

VOICE:
MALE: deep, loud grunting and shouting.
FEMALE: high-pitched squawk and incessant chattering sound.
JUVENILE: Extremely noisy, loud screaming and whining.

HABITAT:
Common almost everywhere. Breeds in noisy, very crowded colonies. Easily located by noise and smell.

Bogies rarely cry, but at times of emotional crisis their Nasal Drip Rate increases dramatically. Normal rate is 30 - 40 drips per minute. In moments of emotional tension this increases to 100 - 120 drips per minute. Occasionally, a continuous flow ensues and upwards of 3 pints of mucus has been collected. This is, of course, watery colourless mucus, not thick green snot.

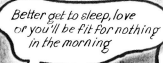

And so we say Farewell to Fungus as he lies awake pondering upon The Significance of His Rôle in Society, Evolution and LIFE....

Meanwhile, all over Bogeydom, the dim light is once more penetrating THE TUNNELS.... The Bogeymen are drawing tight their sticky blinds and climbing into their slimy beds..... SO, FEAR NOT THE BOGEYMAN BY DAY BUT, AT NIGHT.. WATCH OUT!

THE END

THE BOGEY

The last charge,...he lives
A dirty life. Here I could shelter him
With noble and right-reverend precedents,
And show by sanction of authority
That 'tis a very honourable thing
To thrive by dirty ways. But let me rest
On better ground the unanswerable defence.
The Bogey is a philosopher, who knows
No prejudice. Dirt ?... 'Cleaner, what is dirt?
If matter,....why the delicate dish that tempts
An o'ergorged Epicure to the last morsel
That stuffs him to the throat-gates, is no more.
If matter be not, but as Sages say,
Spirit is all, and all things visible
Are one, the infinitely modified,
Think, 'Cleaner, what that Bogey is, and the mire
Wherein he stands knee-deep!

ROBERT SOUTHEY

Some other picture books by Raymond Briggs

FATHER CHRISTMAS
FATHER CHRISTMAS GOES ON HOLIDAY
JIM AND THE BEANSTALK
THE SNOWMAN
THE SNOWMAN STORY BOOK

Some picture books illustrated by Raymond Briggs

THE ADVENTURES OF BERT   *Allan Ahlberg*
A BIT MORE BERT   *Allan Ahlberg*
THE ELEPHANT AND THE BAD BABY   *Elfrida Vipont*

PENGUIN BOOKS

Published by the Penguin Group
Penguin Books Ltd, 80 Strand, London WC2R 0RL, England
Penguin Group (USA), Inc., 375 Hudson Street, New York, New York 10014, USA
Penguin Books Australia Ltd, 250 Camberwell Road, Camberwell, Victoria 3124, Australia
Penguin Books Canada Ltd, 10 Alcorn Avenue, Toronto, Ontario, Canada M4V 3B2
Penguin Books India (P) Ltd, 11 Community Centre, Panchsheel Park, New Delhi – 110 017, India
Penguin Group (NZ), cnr Airborne and Rosedale Roads, Albany, Auckland 1310, New Zealand
Penguin Books (South Africa) (Pty) Ltd, 24 Sturdee Avenue, Rosebank 2196, South Africa

Penguin Books Ltd, Registered Offices: 80 Strand, London WC2R 0RL, England

www.penguin.com

First published by Hamish Hamilton Ltd 1977
Published in Picture Puffins 1990
Reprinted in Penguin Books 1993
25 27 29 30 28 26 24

Copyright © Raymond Briggs, 1977
All rights reserved

Made and printed in Singapore by Tien Wah Press (Pte) Ltd

British Library Cataloguing in Publication Data
A CIP catalogue record for this book is available from the British Library

0–140–54235–3